Mel Bay's Blues Keyboard Method, Level 1

An Essential Study of Blues PIANO and ORGAN for the Novice Player

By Steve Czarnecki & David Barrett

School of the Blues Lesson Series

CD contents

1 Ex. 1.10	14 Ex. 2.11	26 Ex. 3.11	38 Ex. 4.3	50 Chords	
2 Ex. 1.27	15 Ex. 2.12	27 Ex. 3.12	39 Ex. 4.4	51 Gospel 1	
3 Ex. 1.48	16 Ex. 3.1	28 Ex. 3.13	40 Ex. 4.5	52 Gospel 2	
4 Ex. 2.1	17 Ex. 3.2	29 Ex. 3.14	41 Ex. 4.6	53 Diagonal	
5 Ex. 2.2	18 Ex. 3.3	30 Ex. 3.15	42 Ex. 4.7	54 Curved	
6 Ex. 2.3	19 Ex. 3.4	31 Ex. 3.16	43 Jimmy Smith	55 Full Organ	
7 Ex. 2.4	20 Ex. 3.5	32 Ex. 3.17	44 Groove Holmes	56 Change from Jazz to Full Organ	
8 Ex. 2.5	21 Ex. 3.6	33 Ex. 3.18	45 Booker T. 1	57 Ex. 5.1	
9 Ex. 2.6	22 Ex. 3.7	34 Ex. 3.19	46 Booker T. 2	58 Ex. 5.2	
10 Ex. 2.7	23 Ex. 3.8	35 Ex. 3.20	47 Rock	59 Ex. 5.3	
11 Ex. 2.8	24 Ex. 3.9	36 Ex. 4.1	48 Jazz	60 Ex. 5.4	
12 Ex. 2.9	25 Ex. 3.10	37 Ex. 4.2	49 Squabble	61 Common Organ Techniques	
13 Ex. 2.10					

1 2 3 4 5 6 7 8 9 0

© 2006 BY MEL BAY PUBLICATIONS, INC., PACIFIC, MO 63069.
ALL RIGHTS RESERVED. INTERNATIONAL COPYRIGHT SECURED. B.M.I. MADE AND PRINTED IN U.S.A.
No part of this publication may be reproduced in whole or in part, or stored in a retrieval system, or transmitted in any form
or by any means, electronic, mechanical, photocopy, recording, or otherwise, without written permission of the publisher.

Visit us on the Web at www.melbay.com — E-mail us at email@melbay.com

Table of Contents

About The Author & School of the Blues Lesson Series – Track 1 3
Chapter 1 – Music Primer 4
   Understanding Music Notation (Ex. 1.1-1.16) 4
   Understanding Music Theory 7
      Intervals (Ex. 1.17) – Track 1 7
      Scales (Ex. 1.18-20) 7
      Chords (Ex. 1.21-1.32) – Tracks 1-2 7
      Dominant 7th Scales (Ex. 1.33-1.36) – Track 2 11
      Inversions (Ex. 1.37-1.47) 13
      12 Bar Blues Progression (Ex. 1.48-1.49) – Track 3 16
Chapter 2 – Two-Handed Blues - 12 Bar Music Examples (Ex. 2.1-2.12) – Tracks 4-15 18
Chapter 3 – Improvising in the Blues 27
   Harmonic Elements – Blues Scales (Ex. 3.1-3.2) – Tracks 16-17 27
   Structural Improvisation (Ex. 3.3-3.14) – Tracks 18-29 28
   Chorus Forms (Ex. 3.15-3.20) – Tracks 30-35 32
Chapter 4 – Openings, Endings & Breaks 39
   Openings (Ex. 4.1-4.2) – Tracks 36-37 39
   Breaks (Ex. 4.3-4.4) – Tracks 38-39 39
   Endings (Ex. 4.5-4.7) – Tracks 40-42 40
Chapter 5 – Blues Organ 42
   Typical Drawbar Settings – Tracks 43-56 43
   Organ Music Examples (Ex. 5.1-5.4) – Tracks 57-60 44
   Organ Techniques (Ex. 5.5-5.8) – Track 61 46
Final Thoughts, Recommended Listening & Thanks To 47

About This Method

This book in the *School of the Blues Lesson Series* is aimed toward the beginning to intermediate pianist interested in learning to play the Blues. This book is organized in the following way:

We'll first start with a brief review of some piano basics. The names of the notes on the Treble and Bass Clefs, rhythmic values of notes on the staff, information about the musical concept of keys, fingering for scales and stylistic aspects of the Blues as it relates to the keyboard.

The second section presents a series of two-handed exercises in the 12 Bar Blues form. I've found that a lot of keyboard students will spend the majority of their time playing and practicing by themselves rather than in a group context. The great strength of the piano is in its ability to be a whole band. I'll present a number of left hand accompaniment patterns for you to try. You'll also learn some right hand melodies for improvisation that will draw from basic musical ideas and scale patterns. By mixing and matching these set elements in both hands, you can be playing Blues in no time!

The third section covers the development of musical ideas in the right hand over the 12 bar Blues progression. With one or two right hand phrases you can, through repetition and variation, create authentic sounding Blues solos, chorus after chorus.

The fourth section will show you how to play openings, breaks and endings when performing with other musicians.

The fifth section deals with Blues as it's played on the Hammond organ. You might think the piano and organ are virtually the same instrument, but in reality they are two entirely different instruments that share only one characteristic—a keyboard. I'll show you various approaches to using the organ in Blues.

About the Author

Steve Czarnecki plays piano and Hammond organ in the San Francisco Bay Area and is a respected member of the local music community. He has released four CDs under his own name on the PMP label as well as multiple recording projects for other artists.

When I Dream of You and *Sunnyside Up* showcase Steve's jazz piano skills. The *Soul/Jazz Quintet* features Steve's Hammond organ chops along with vocalist Nate Pruitt, also a teacher at the School of the Blues. *Soul Rendezvous* is his latest CD and features Steve's original compositions.

Steve has worked and played with many musicians in his career including Robben Ford, Mark Ford, Ernie Watts, Alphonse Mouzon, Barney Kessel, Kenny Rankin, John Garcia, Charlie Musselwhite and others. His current group, Steve Czarnecki's Soul/Jazz Quintet, performs in the San Francisco Bay Area. He's also a member of the School of the Blues All-Star Band. He can be reached at www.soul-jazz.com.

About the School of the Blues Lesson Series

School of the Blues is a school dedicated to the study of Blues and all the styles it influenced. Founded in 2002 by educator David Barrett, the school thrives today as the center of Blues education in the San Jose/San Francisco, California Bay Area.

The instructors at the school and this lesson series have on average twenty years teaching and performing experience. All of the instructors were hand picked to teach at the school for their playing skills, knowledge of their instrument and ability to teach all skill levels of private and group instruction. We're all dedicated to our craft and receive huge pleasure playing an active role in our students' musical and personal development as well rounded musicians.

This series is a continuation of this love for the Blues and its education. David Barrett is the administrator and coauthor of all the books. Many meetings took place with the instructors to shape the outline of this lesson series and to make sure that the experience and knowledge of the instructors are contained within each book.

This series is also designed for students of other instruments to play together. If you have friends that play harmonica, guitar, bass or drums, tell them about this series so that you can grow together. There's nothing more fun than making music with other people.

We all wish you the best of luck in your studies. For more information about this series or to contact us, please visit www.schooloftheblues.com.

Chapter 1 – Music Primer

Understanding Music Notation

We all come to the piano with different experience and abilities. Some have taken the standard "classical" piano lessons of childhood, and others may be approaching the instrument with musical experience learned on another instrument, or perhaps no previous musical experience at all, just a desire to play. Therefore, I'm going to cover some basic material to make sure we're all starting at the same place. While some people can play well without reading music, the only way to really take advantage of all the musical knowledge that exists is having the ability to decipher musical notation. You notice I didn't say "read" music. For this book, all you need to be able to do is know which note is to be played when. As long as you can do this, and remember what you have learned, then you'll be fine. Reading music, as in sight-reading music, like reading to someone from a book, is not necessary here. This is a quick overview. As you walk through this book these concepts will be presented again, accompanied by the recording so that you can hear them in context.

Staff: The music staff has five lines. Time moves from left to right on the staff.

Ex. 1.1

Ledger Lines: The lower lines hold notes that are low in pitch. The upper lines hold notes that are high in pitch. Sometimes notes go beyond the five lines and ledger lines are used to help keep your place.

Ex. 1.2

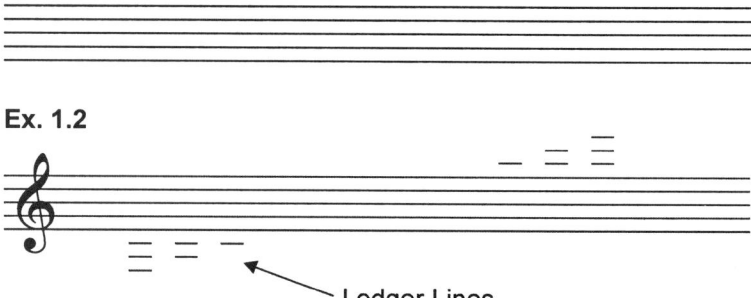

Treble Clef: The treble clef symbol is placed at the beginning of a staff to give a reference pitch. You can see that the bottom curl encircles the second line from the bottom. This second line is the pitch G. Because of this, the treble clef is also known as the **G Clef.**

Ex. 1.3

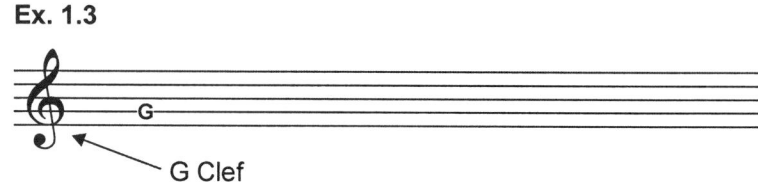

Notes on the Line: Notes are found on each line of the staff and ledger lines. The notes **E G B D F** found on the staff can be remembered by using "**E**very **G**ood **B**oy **D**oes **F**ine."

Ex. 1.4

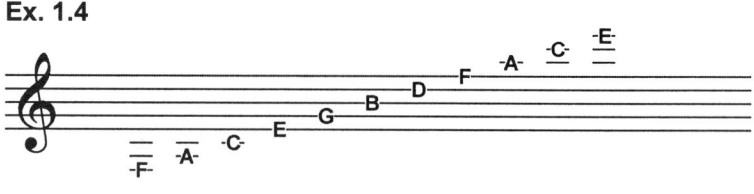

Notes in the Spaces: Notes are also found in the spaces. The notes **F A C E** found on the staff can be remembered by using "**FACE.**"

Ex. 1.5

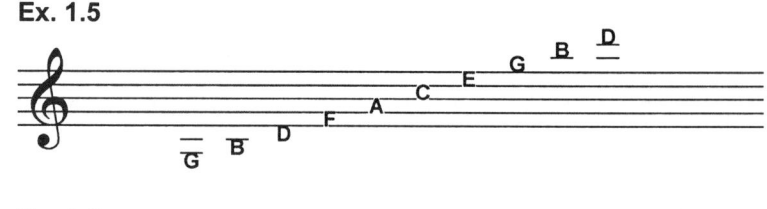

Stem Direction: Notes are placed on these lines and spaces that tell you how long to hold a note. You will see notes that have stems. Some stems point upward and some stems point downward. Stem direction does not change the pitch or length of a note.

Ex. 1.6

Time Signature, Bar Line & Ending: The line that dissects the staff is called a ***Bar Line***. The time between two bar lines is called a ***Measure***. The thin bar line and thick bar line at the end of the staff tells you that the song is over. The ***Time Signature*** is placed at the beginning of a piece of music to tell you how many beats are in a measure and which note duration is to receive the beat. The 4/4 time signature shows that there are four beats per measure and the quarter note receives the beat.

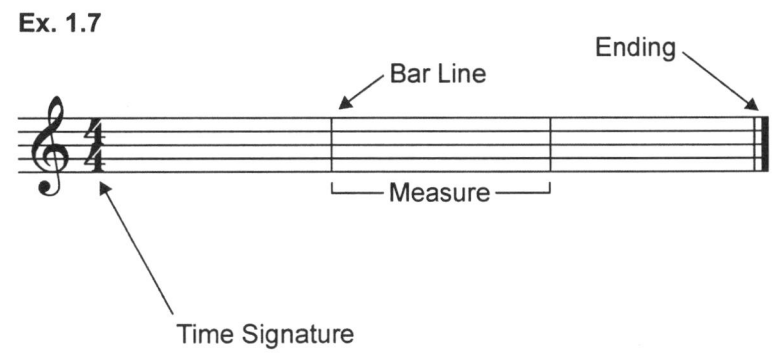

Ex. 1.7

The musical staff is divided into two parts for piano—the ***Treble Staff*** and the ***Bass Staff***. The treble staff (indicated by the treble clef) contains notes that will be played with your right hand. The bass staff contains the notes played by your left hand. For the treble staff the spaces are (from bottom to top) F-A-C-E. The lines are E-G-B-D-F. The bass clef is shifted down by one space or line: the spaces are A-C-E-G and the lines are G-B-D-F-A.

Ex. 1.8

Note Durations: A whole note is held for a count of four beats, or one whole measure. A half note is held for a count of two beats, or half a measure. A quarter note is held for one beat, or one quarter of a measure.

Pitch & Duration on the Staff: This example shows: the 4/4 time signature; a C whole note for the first measure; a C half note and A half note for the second measure; and B, A, G, and F quarter notes for the third measure.

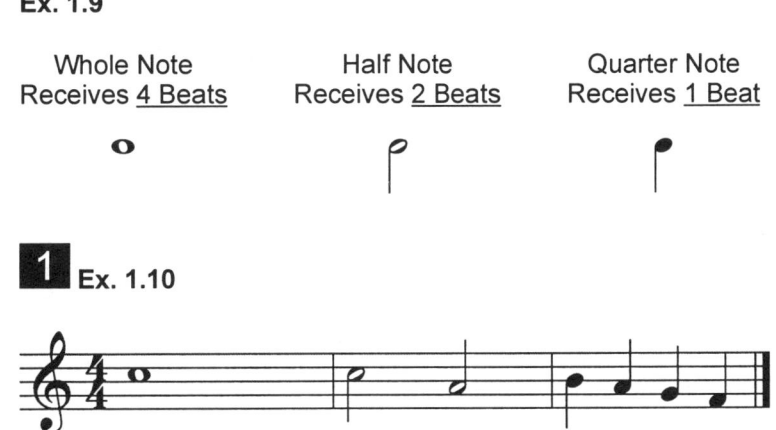

Ex. 1.9

The example below demonstrates the common rhythms we'll use that subdivide the beat. The example starts with quarter notes to show that each quarter note lands on the beat. To the right of the quarter note is the eighth note, which has two notes per beat (each worth a half beat). The sixteenth rhythm is four notes to the beat (each worth one quarter of a beat). The triplet rhythm is three notes to the beat (each worth a third of a beat).

Ex. 1.11

When a dot is added to a note, it extends its value by half. A half note with a dot equals three beats and a quarter note with a dot equals a beat and a half. All notes have a corresponding rest. When seeing these, you will not play. This is shown below.

Ex. 1.12

You may notice that many Blues pieces have a bouncy or swinging kind of rhythm. While they may be written like this:

Ex. 1.13

To achieve the correct swinging feel, they would actually be played like this:

Ex. 1.14

This can also be expressed in 12/8 time.

Ex. 1.15

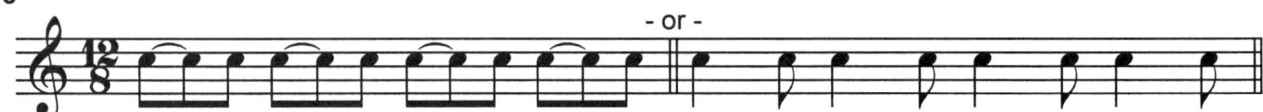

Because of the awkwardness of reading music written this way, when you see eighth notes, play them swung unless specified otherwise. Focus on each downbeat eighth note being longer in time and upbeat eighth notes shorter and slightly later in time. This will give us the swing feel we're looking for. Below is a simple example to get accustomed to this feel.

Ex. 1.16

Understanding Music Theory

To understand how Blues works, let's take a moment and talk about scales, intervals and chords.

Interval

An Interval is the distance between two notes. The smallest distance between two notes is the *Half Step* (also known as a *Semi-Tone*) such as C to C#. From these half steps larger intervals, scales and chords are constructed. Below is the *Chromatic Scale* from C to C using sharps. This scale is made up entirely of half steps. You can't fit any note between any two successive notes of the scale. This scale can also be constructed using flats (C# turns into D♭, D# turns into E♭, etc.).

Ex. 1.17

Scales

Most American music works within the diatonic system. *Diatonic* denotes a scale that uses two half steps and five whole steps for its construction. A *Whole Step* is created when playing two notes separated by two half steps (such as C to D). Below is the C Major scale. A *Major Scale* places a half step between the third and fourth notes in the scale, commonly referred to as *Scale Degrees*. A second half step occurs between the seventh and eighth scale degrees.

Ex. 1.18

Following this system of whole steps and half steps you can create a major scale from any staring note. Demonstrated below is the E♭ major scale.

Ex. 1.19

From these scales, melodies can be made. Demonstrated below is a melody using the C major scale.

Ex. 1.20

Chords

What are chords? For our purpose, a *Chord* is any group of three or more notes played simultaneously. Usually they're built upon intervals of a third or fourth. How are they made? Let's take the C major scale. To build a chord, start with a note from the scale and build in thirds. This is demonstrated in Example 1.21. The numbers below the notes designate their position in the scale.

Ex. 1.21

To make a **I** (one) chord, start with the first note of the scale (position 1) and build in thirds. Skip the D and play the E, skip the F and play the G and stop. The **I** chord notes are C-E-G. C is the root of the chord. E is the third of the chord (third note from the root). G is the fifth of the chord. You can continue up the chord, but let's stick with what is called a ***Triad*** (grouping of three notes in thirds).

Ex. 1.22

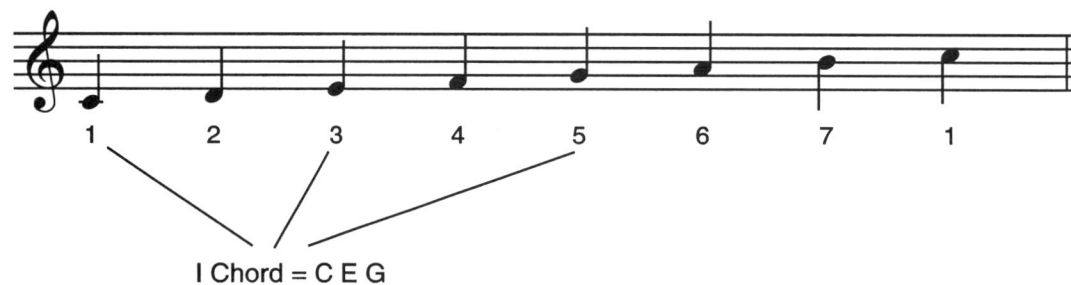

Following the same procedure for all of the notes will give you all seven chords.

Ex. 1.23

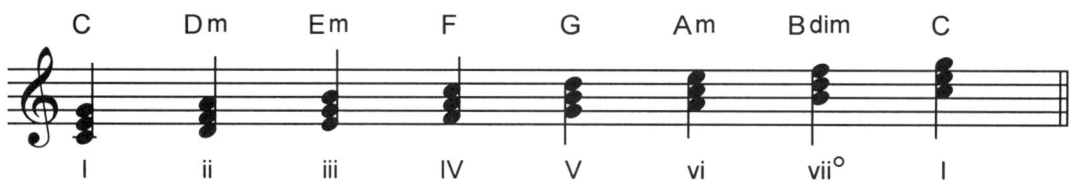

These are all the chords in the key of C. From this set of chords you can find a chord to accompany any note in a melody in the key of C.

Now let's look at each chord individually. The first chord is built from the note C and is therefore called a C chord (**I**), specifically a ***C Major Chord***. Why is it Major? The interval between the bottom note (C) and the next higher note (E) is a major third (4 half steps). Demonstrated below is a table of intervals for our reference.

Ex. 1.24

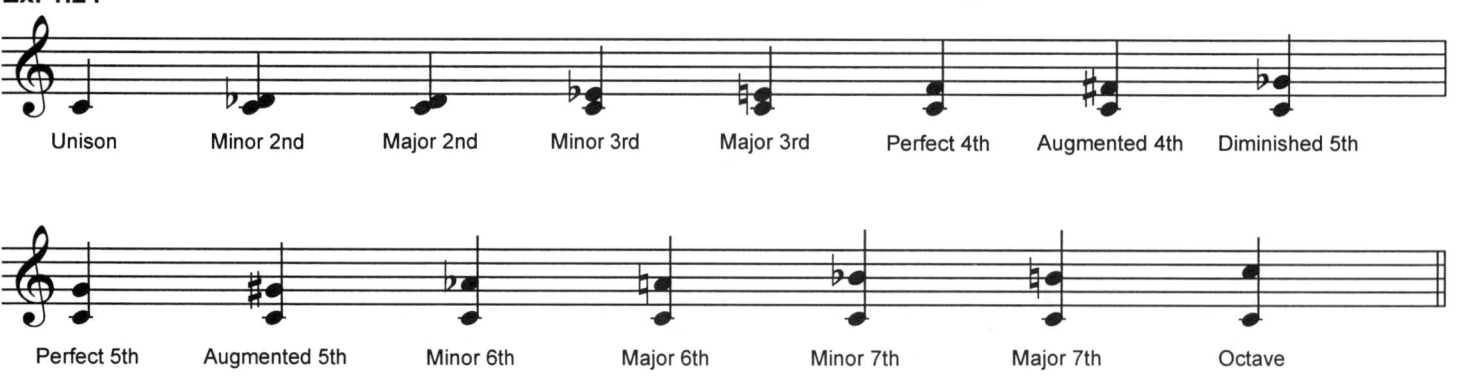

This major third gives the chord its bright sound. If we look closely at the other chords we see that the chords built on F (**IV**) and on G (**V**) are major chords as well. We can tell this by the sound and the fact that the interval between the root note and the next higher note is a major third (4 half steps).

Let's examine the second chord (**ii**) in the Scale. This chord is built from D. The interval between the root and the next higher note is 3 half steps—a minor third. When we play this chord we notice it has a darker sound. This is characteristic of minor chords. This is a D Minor chord. There are two other minor chords in the key of C: The chord with E (**iii**) as its root and the chord with A (**vi**) as its root.

So far in the key of C (and in all other Major keys), we've found three major chords and three minor chords. There is one chord left. Built upon the B is a chord with a minor third interval between the root and the next note, but as we play it, we hear that it is much different from the other minor chords. This difference lies in the interval made between the root and the top note. In all the other chords this is a perfect fifth (7 half steps); here it is a diminished fifth (6 half steps). We won't be using this chord in this book, so you needn't worry about it now. Just become familiar with the sound.

Now, with these chords we can harmonize any melody in the key of C.

Ex. 1.25

We can make up a chord progression (series of chords) in the key of C as well. Just try it. Start with a C chord, randomly go through other chords (you may repeat some if you wish) and don't play the C chord till the very end.

Ex. 1.26

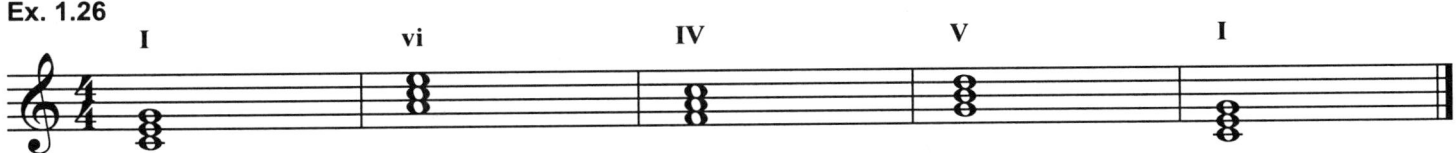

Under or over each of the chords from the previous examples there are Roman numerals representing their chord qualities. Upper case Roman numeral (**I**) represents a **Major Chord**. A lower case Roman numeral (**i**) represents a **Minor Chord**. A lower case Roman numeral with a small circle (**i°**) represents a **Diminished Chord**. You'll see these designations throughout the book.

Now let's tie this to the blues.

The harmonic system above was developed over centuries by western European musicians. It forms the basis of what we call classical and popular music today. The Blues however, has a different story. With arrival of black slaves in the new world, a different musical tradition was added to the musical mix. African music does not share the same harmonic concepts as European music. In general, it is less developed in this area while being much more advanced than its counterpart in the field of rhythm. When these two collided, both were changed for the better. The harmony we use in the Blues is a combination of European harmonic elements bent to an African esthetic. To complete our harmonic picture, we'll need to add another note to the top of our new chords. See the example below.

2 Ex. 1.27

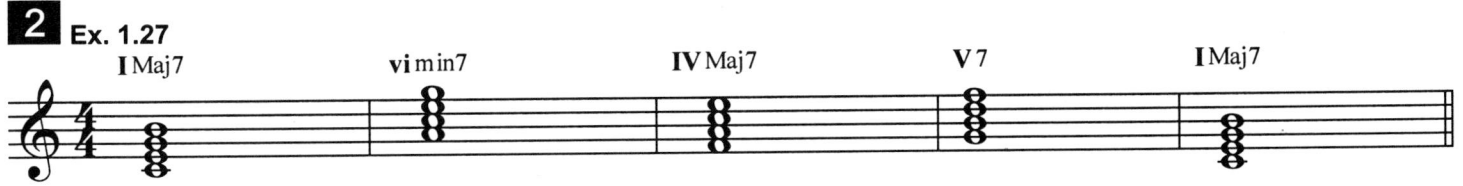

As you can see, I've added another note (B) above the G in our C Major chord. This chord is now a **C Major 7th Chord**. The 7th refers to the interval between the root C and the top note B (11 half steps). Just so you know, you can keep adding notes a third above to this chord. You'll get a **C Major 9th Chord**, **C Major 11th Chord** and finally a **C Major 13th Chord**. At this point we're at the end of our C Major universe (and probably the end of our wits, too). We've used up all the notes in the C scale to build out this C chord to its complete extension!

Ex. 1.28

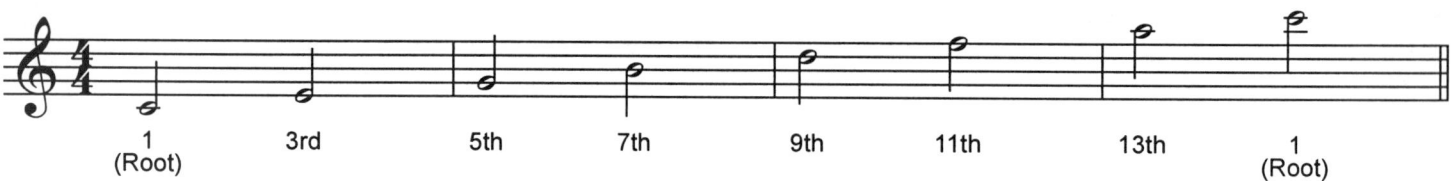

Now, back to earth. If we do this same process with the other chords in the key of C we get similarly extended chords. But for the blues, the only one we need to concentrate on is the chord built on G. When we add one extra note above the D we get a **G Dominant 7th Chord**. Let's stop here.

Ex. 1.29

This is the most important chord in the blues. If you know this chord you can play 80% of all blues tunes. Since it's so important, let's take a closer look. Why isn't this chord a G Major 7th, like the C Major 7th? They both are built from Major chords. What differentiates the Dominant 7th from the C Major 7th is the interval between the bottom and top notes.

Ex. 1.30

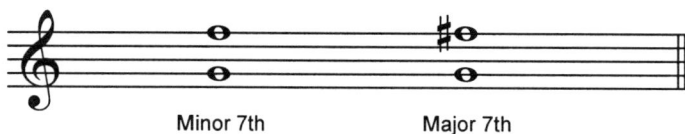

In our Dominant 7th chord the interval between the root and the seventh is a minor 7th (10 half steps). This chord is the backbone of the Blues. In a typical popular song in the key of C, we would find most of the chords in that key used this for the accompaniment. Our G chord (or G Dominant 7th chord) would most likely come right before the final C chord. See the example below. We've all heard this sound. It's very common in all the music we hear.

Ex. 1.31

Let's now take a look at a typical 12 Bar Blues Progression. This is demonstrated on the following page.

Ex. 1.32

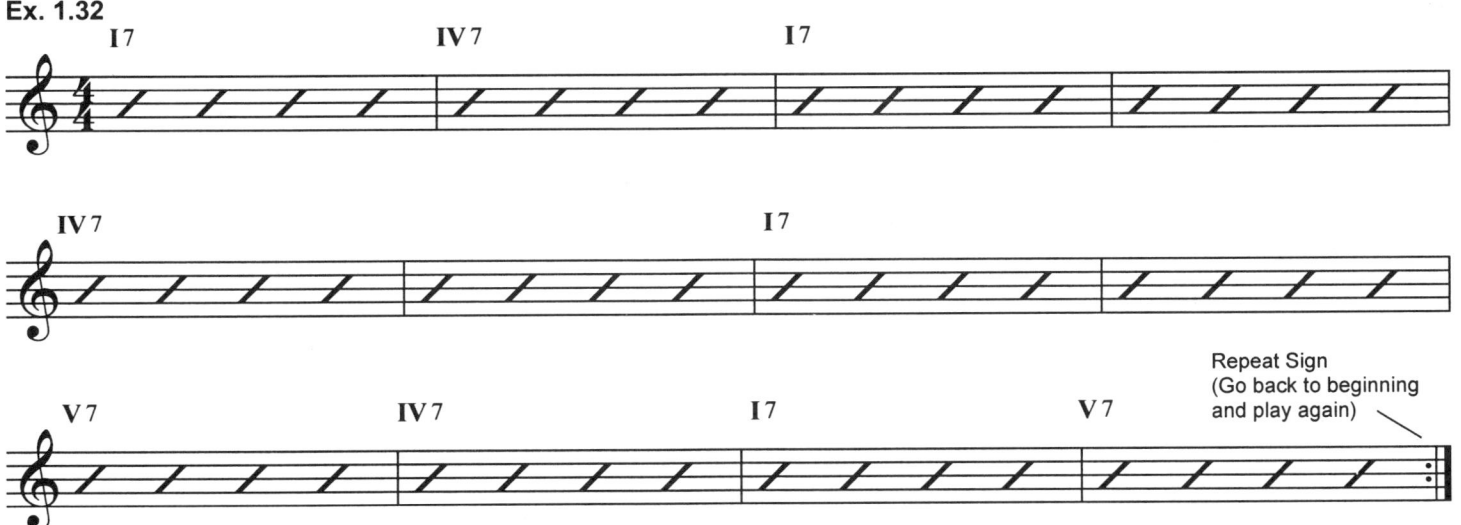

Notice that all the chords are Dominant 7th chords. If this progression were written as a standard pop or even classical progression, we would expect only the G chord in the 10th bar to be a Dominant 7th. In Blues, all the chords are Dominant 7th. This is part of what gives the Blues its distinct sound.

Now that we see the importance of the Dominant 7th chord, what scale can we use to make melodies over theses chords? If this were a typical non-blues progression the answer would be easy, the notes in the C Major scale. In the case of our blues progression, however, we'll need to alter our Major scale to accommodate the flat 7th of the Dominant 7th chord.

Ex. 1.33

Now, for the F7 Chord, we'll take an F Major scale and flat its 7th.

Ex. 1.34

Now, finally, we'll have to alter the G Major scale to accommodate the flatted 7th. Wait a minute! It has already been done. In the key of C playing the C Major scale from G to G gives us the G dominant 7th scale. The G7 chord in the Blues Progression is the only one being use in a traditional non-Blues fashion.

Ex. 1.35

So, you can see why blues is such a distinctive music, just from a harmonic perspective. It plays with the rules of European harmony, keeping some rules and altering others to its taste. On the following page are all the **Dominant 7th Scales** with correct fingering for the right hand.

Ex. 1.36

Inversions

Let's take chords another step forward. Below is our typical 12 Bar Blues Progression in the key of C with the chords written in for you.

Ex. 1.37

As you can see, the C7, F7 and G7 chords are all here. The only problem is that to play these chords you have to do a lot of jumping around on the keyboard. In general, a lot of excessive moving about when playing chords does not create the best music. Now look at this version of the 12 Bar Blues.

Ex. 1.38

The C7 chord is the same, but the F7 and G7 chords look different. The notes are the same as the previous example, but they have been rearranged. This rearranging of the notes in a chord creates a different version of the chord called an **Inversion**.

The C7 chord as we've studied before has C at the bottom followed by E, G and B♭. This is called a **Root Position Chord**. If I take the C from the bottom and move it up an octave, we get what's notated in the next example.

Ex. 1.39

This is the *1st Inversion* of the C7 chord. It retains the same general sound and function of our original, or root position version of the C7, but is now called the 1st Inversion of the C7 chord. Let's continue this process. Next I'll take the E, which is now the lowest note, and move it up an octave. Now we have the **2nd Inversion** of the C7 chord.

Ex. 1.40

If we take the G and move it up an octave, the B♭ is now our lowest note for the *3rd Inversion*. This is the final inversion of the C7 chord.

Ex. 1.41

I'll write out all these chords in succession. They actually make a good exercise to become comfortable with the various inversions of the Dominant 7th chords. Here, we can do the same for the F7 and G7 as well.

Ex. 1.42

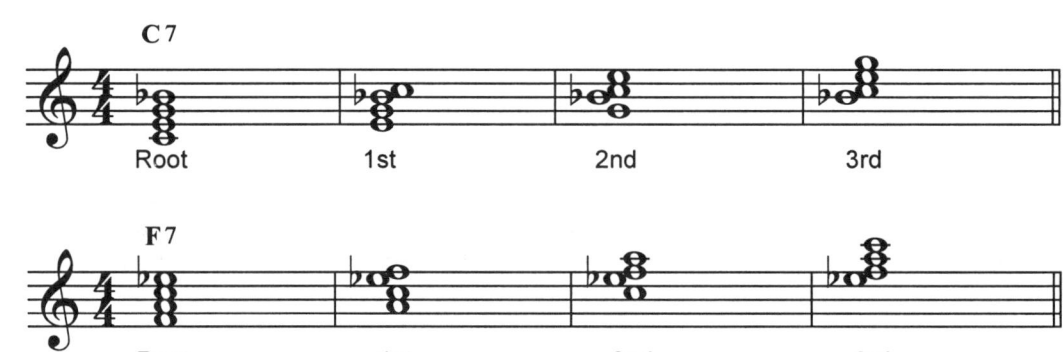

Ex. 1.43

Ex. 1.44

So, the general rule is, the notes of any chord can be inverted (rearranged) as many times as there are notes in the chord. A Triad can only be rearranged three times: Root Position, 1st Inversion and 2nd Inversion. A four-note chord, such as our G7 will have the root position and 3 inversions (four different ways to play the chord).

Below are several exercises on the C Blues. In each one we'll start on a different version of the C7 chord. The best musical results will occur if we can keep our hand from jumping around on the keyboard. In each exercise I've tried to keep each successive chord as close to the position of that preceding it.

Demonstrated on the next page is the 12 Bar Blues Progression starting with the C chord in its *1st Inversion*. In this inversion the 3rd of each chord is the lowest sounding note.

Ex. 1.45

Demonstrated below is the 12 Bar Blues Progression starting with the C chord in its **2nd Inversion**. In this inversion the 5th of each chord is the lowest sounding note.

Ex. 1.46

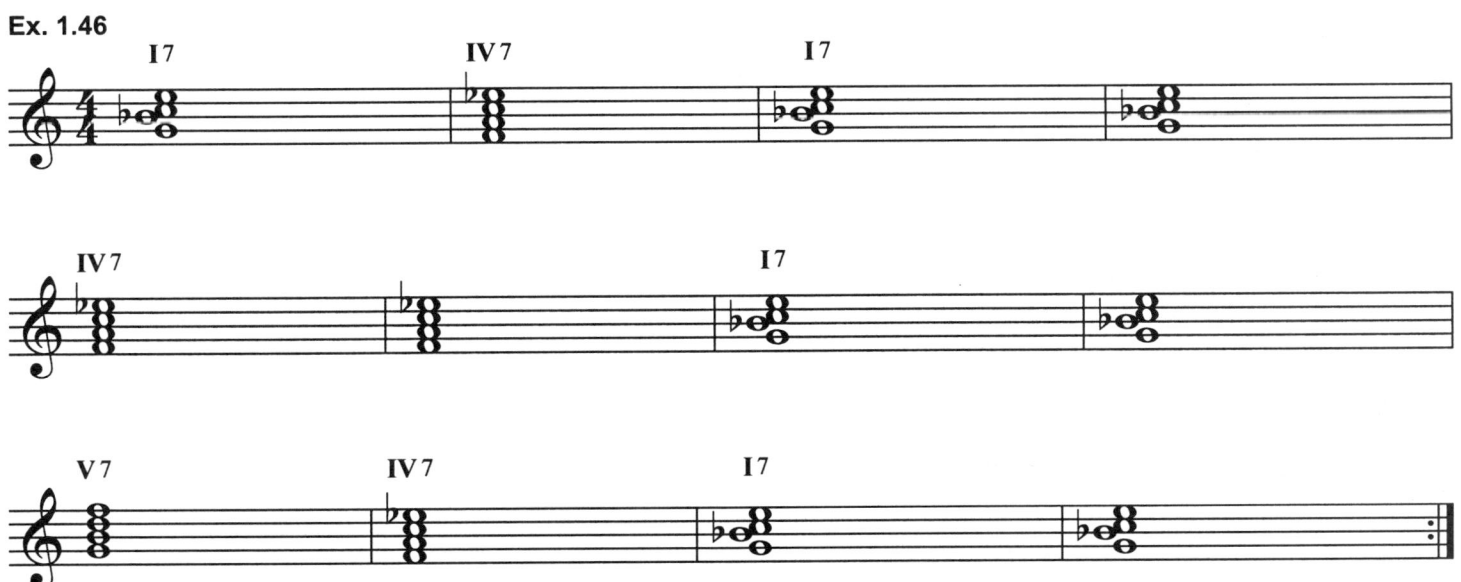

Demonstrated below is the 12 Bar Blues Progression starting with the C chord in its **3rd Inversion**. In this inversion the 7th of each chord is the lowest sounding note.

Ex. 1.47

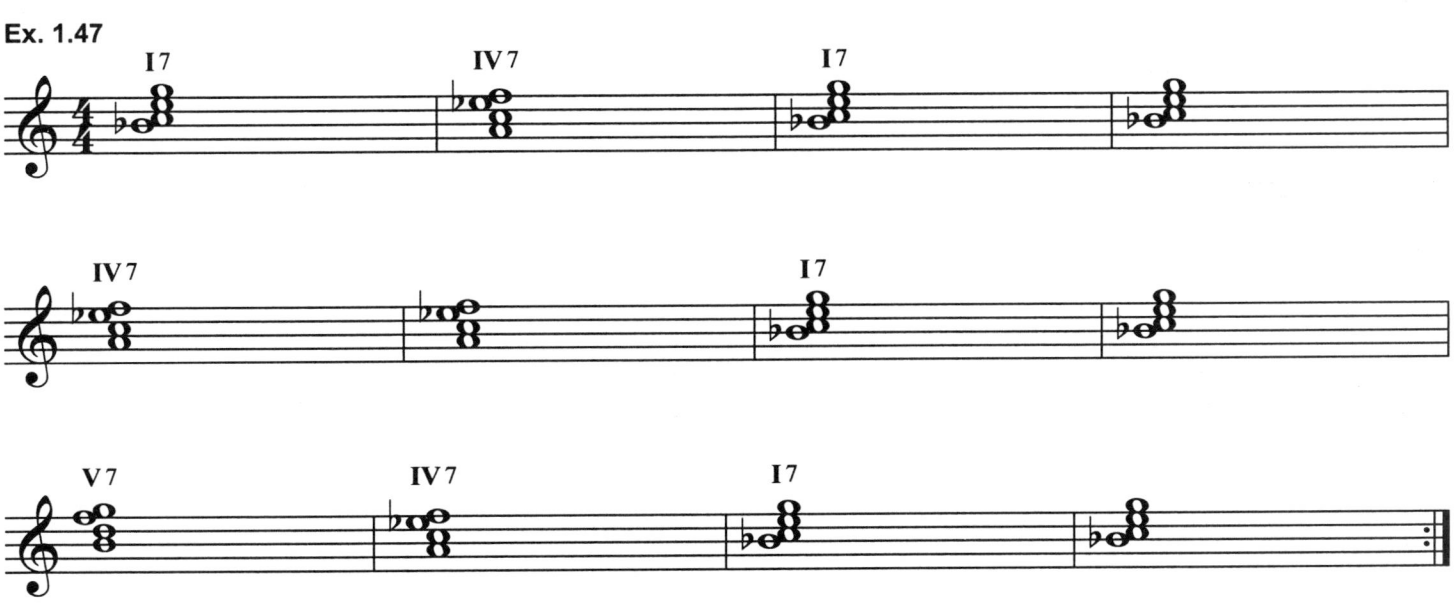

The 12 Bar Blues Form

In general, the Blues is a 12 Bar Form. This means one complete chorus of Blues in 4/4 time will start on bar one and end at the fourth beat of bar 12. There is also an 8 Bar Blues, but 95% of the time, and for purposes of this book, we'll be dealing with the standard 12 Bar Blues.

The Blues is unique in its harmonic structure. First, the Blues uses almost exclusively Dominant 7th chords (except when in a minor key, but we won't be dealing with that here). In all other tonal music (classical, pop, jazz, etc.) this limitation is not the case. They will also use major and minor chords. The persistent use of the Dominant 7th is an essential characteristic of Blues music.

There are basically two types of 12 Bar Blues Progressions—Long Change and Quick Change. The **Long Change** form uses the **I7** chord (C7 in the key of C) for four measures in the beginning of the form, where the **Short Change** uses the **IV7** chord at the second measure, returning to the **I7** at the third measure. One time through the 12 Bar Blues Progression is called one **Chorus** (or one **Verse** if you are singing). The form will repeat until the song is over (commonly six to nine choruses depending on the tempo of the song). This is demonstrated below.

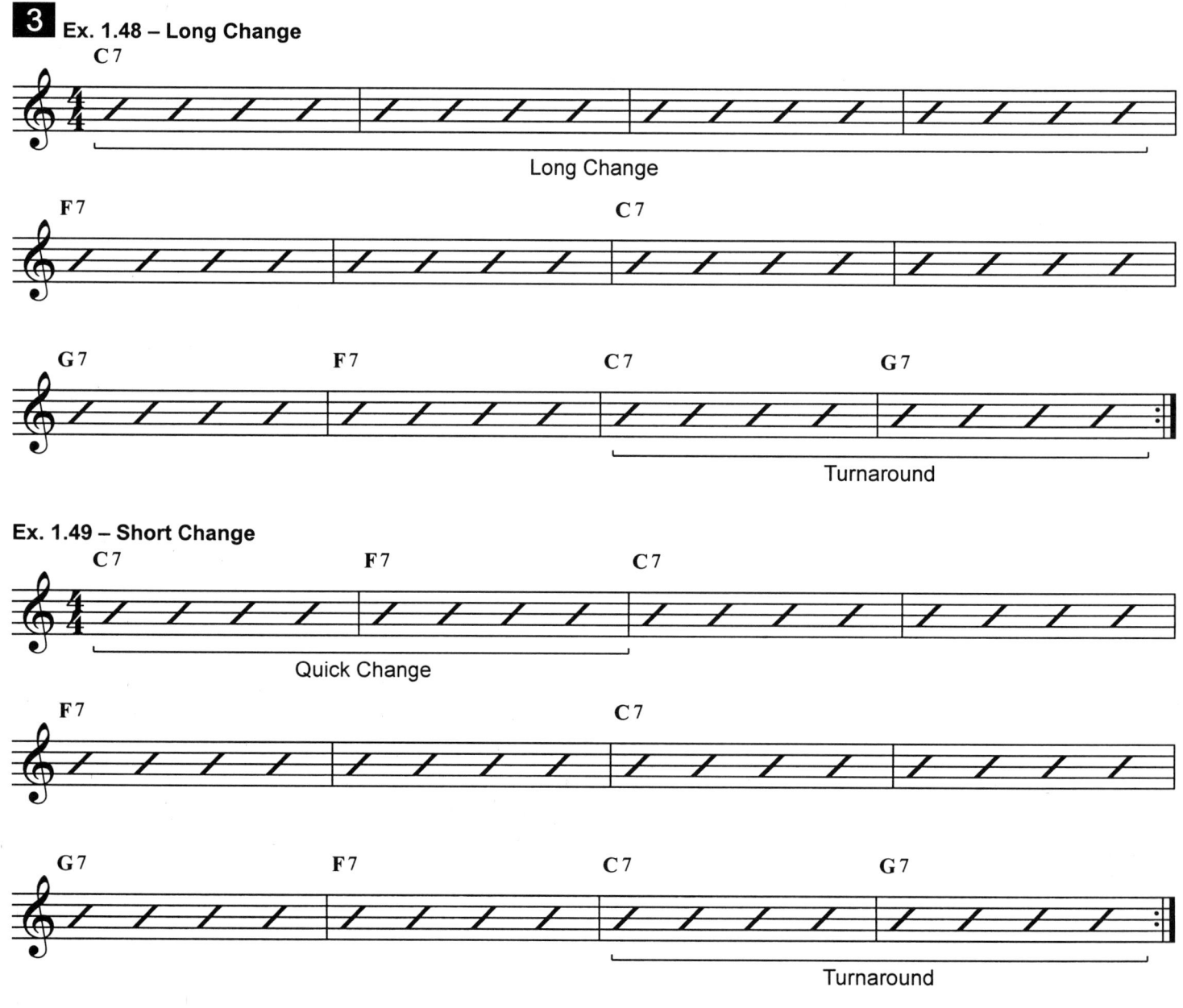

16

It's also common to have the **IV7** chord in bar 10 to be replaced with a continuation of the **V7** chord. These variations (long changes, short changes and use of the V7 chord for two measures at measure 9) may appear separately, together or not at all.

The ***Turnaround***, located at the last two measures of the form, helps to tell the listener that the progression is going to repeat. What makes the turnaround is the **V7** in the last measure. Depending on the lick that you play, the **V7** can happen anywhere in time within that last measure. Keep in mind that in some songs the turnaround is not used. In that case, the **I7** is used for all of the last two measures. We'll see examples of both in the coming text.

Chapter 2 – **Two-Handed Blues**

The following are simple exercises in the 12 bar Blues form. Your goal is to be able to play through each exercise at least twice with a steady tempo. After you feel comfortable with an exercise, you may add a chorus or more of improvisation between the initial and final written choruses. When doing this, your left hand will play the same part, with the right hand providing the new improvised material. Feel free to use either, or both of the Blues scales mentioned in Chapter 3, the Dominant 7th Scales mentioned in Chapter 1, or anything that sounds good to you. It's important however, no matter what you play, that the beat remains rock steady—particularly in the left hand throughout.

If we look at Example 2.1, we see that it's smooth sailing through the end of bar four. Keeping steady time should be no problem up to this point. But, the change from beat four of measure four to the first beat of measure five involves a big jump in the left hand. This happens again between measures six and seven, eight and nine, ten and eleven, and twelve back to one (you can keep repeating the exercise as many times as you wish). These are the trouble spots in performing these examples. Since they are much more challenging than the other bars, perhaps we should have some kind of strategy to deal with them. Here's an approach borrowed from classical music.

Let's take the jump from the C-G left hand part in bar four to the F-C part in bar five. First, let's isolate the problem: the left hand jump. The idea here is to practice slowly to play quickly. Play the C-G, then move your hand slowly up to the F-C and play it. Do this again three more times slowly. No, slower than that! I mean <u>slowly</u>. Now gradually speed up this motion. Three more times at a medium speed. Now, let's do it up to tempo. Now, let's move back one beat. We'll play the C-G from beat three and then the F-C ending on beat two. We're expanding our problem area by one beat on both sides. Play it slowly three times, then faster, and finally up to tempo three times. To finish, let's do this process from the beginning of bar four and ending at the last beat of bar five. By now, you'll be able to make this jump at a reasonable tempo, and won't have to commit the unpardonable crime of slowing down to make the chord change.

You should use this approach for all the other left-hand jumps in this and future exercises, and for any other technically difficult areas in a piece. Once again, recognize the weak or broken spot. Isolate the exact problem. Practice it slowly several times. Move it up in tempo. Expand the practice forward and backward one beat at a time, playing slowly and then up to tempo.

Whatever you do, when you have a problem area or weak spot in a piece, <u>don't stop after the mistake and go back to the beginning</u>. Efficient practice means practicing <u>only</u> what you need to practice. You're wasting time by wading through half a piece just to get to a problem in bar eight.

Example 2.1 is our first exercise. Again, it's a 12 Bar Blues in the Key of C. You'll notice that there's no **V7** chord (G7) at the last measure. This enables you to end here whenever you wish. Take this exercise at a slow enough tempo so that it remains steady. The chords in the right hand are inversions of the C7, F7 and G7 chords. You'll notice I left one note out of each chord, usually the root or fifth. This works because the left hand is providing these notes.

You'll notice as I play these exercises that I sometimes slur into a note on a white key from a black key—from below or above. This extra note comes just before the beat the main note falls on. In this case I'm playing the black key as a grace note. This is the miniature note you'll see notated in front of a note. When this extra note is not specifically notated, I'm using a slide. This is one of the techniques used to add expressiveness to blues piano.

4 Ex. 2.1

Example 2.2 has the same right hand part as Example 2.1. You'll notice, however, that the left hand has changed. The rhythmic values are now eighth notes instead of quarter notes. This is one of the most common left hand patterns.

5 Ex. 2.2

Here's a new left hand part slightly different than that in Example 2.1.

6 Ex. 2.3

For our next example the left hand is the same as in the preceding exercise. The right hand chords are in what is sometimes called the **Charleston Rhythm**. This rhythm is very useful and is a good one to memorize. In this example the **V7** (G7) chord is played for two measures at the 9th measure (omitting the **IV7** chord commonly found on the 10th measure). Also note the **V7** chord (G7) on beat 2 of the last measure. This is common in the Blues and it leads you back to the **I7** (C7) chord at the beginning. Because of this, if you wanted to end the song, you'd need to end this exercise on beat one of the 12th measure.

7 Ex. 2.4

Here's a new bass (or left hand) part. It's more driving than the others, but harder to solo over. Note the right hand chords over the **I7** part. The A in the **I7** chord (C7) replaces the G that would usually be there. The A is a 13th; the chord is now technically a C13.

8 Ex. 2.5

As you listen to me play these examples on the recording, at the 12th measure I will sometimes deviate from what is written. Sometimes I will stop on the downbeat of the 12th measure to give the example a better feel of completion. I basically played what felt musically right at the moment of recording… this is the essence of Blues performance. If you were to play the example over and over (and you probably will), playing what I wrote will insure a nice transition back to the beginning of the form as you repeat.

Also note how I will roll some chords (such as in example 2.9). This is a common piano technique that adds a nice touch to some songs. To roll a chord, start with lowest sounding note of the left hand and play the notes in sequence, from left to right, until all the notes of the chord have sounded. It's up to you and the feel of the song how much delay you want between the notes in your roll.

For our next example the right hand chords are the same as Example 2.1 and 2.2. This example brings a new left hand part.

9 Ex. 2.6

Here we'll use the left hand part from Example 2.6. In the right hand I'm using 6ths (see Interval table). You could call them chord inversions with the middle note removed.

10 Ex. 2.7

Here's a different left hand part. The notes are mostly the same as in Example 2.1, but the rhythm is different.

11 Ex. 2.8

As you may remember, we've been playing these exercises with a swing beat (see page 6) even though they are written in straight eighth notes. These next exercises are written in 12/8 instead of 4/4. That means that the swing feel is explicitly stated in the music. This is necessary when eighth note triplets are part of the rhythm of the piece.

The left hand in Example 2.9 has the same feel as that of Example 2.8, but it's now written in 12/8 time. You may want to take these exercises at a slower tempo than the previous ones.

12 Ex. 2.9

In Example 2.10, the left hand remains the same, but he right hand is more active.

13 Ex. 2.10

Example 2.11 shows an example of the necessity of the 12/8 time signature. Also note the **V7** chord in bar twelve. This carries us back to the beginning, but we can't end here. Try playing a **I7** chord of your own choosing on the "and" of 2 on that last measure for an ending.

14 Ex. 2.11

This is an example of **Jump Swing**. The left hand is playing what the bass player would play. It's called a **Walking Bass**. Instead of the **IV7** chord in bar 9 we have the related chord—**ii7** (Dm7). To end this exercise play beat one of measure one.

15 Ex. 2.12

Chapter 3 – Improvising in the Blues

As you may or may not know, improvisation plays a large role in the Blues. It's also a structural element. Usually in a Blues performance, the first, or first and second choruses of the Blues composition, have a set melody—commonly referred to as the head. When the head has been played there follows a number of 12 bar choruses in which instrumentalists improvise melodies over the underlying chords. This section is called the solo section (or body in an instrumental) and may involve one player or more in sequence, each playing one or more complete Blues choruses. After the solos, the head returns. A Blues composition may have an introduction and perhaps an extended ending, but the basic structure still holds. Diagramed below is how an instrumental may go if it were focused on one instrument. The head is commonly prearranged, with the body improvised in performance.

```
| Head | Chorus | Chorus | Chorus | Chorus | Chorus | Head ||
         |_____|
                            Body
```

Since improvisation plays such a large role in Blues, you may ask, "exactly how do you improvise if you've never done it before?" There are several approaches, some of which may work better for you than others. Although improvisation may seem daunting, there are several organizing principles which make it easier to do once they're understood.

Harmonic Elements

How do you know which note will work and which one won't? Since a basic Blues progression contains only three chords, we might figure out which sets of notes will work with each chord as a start (see Ex 1.33). Another, simpler approach is the use of the **Blues Scale**. Unlike the approach above, the Blues scale relies on the intrinsic force of the arrangement of notes in the scale to overcome any harmonic mismatches it may produce when played over a certain chord. There are two types of Blues scales—the Major Blues Scale and the Minor Blues Scale.

The **Major Blues Scale** is a major scale with the fourth and seventh note of the scale omitted. A lowered third is added for Bluesy effect. This is a very effective scale when playing Blues with a light feel. If you are familiar with the **Major Pentatonic Scale**—this is the same scale with the addition of the lowered third.

Ex. 3.1

The **Minor Blues Scale** is a minor scale with the second and sixth note of the scale omitted. A lowered fifth is added for Bluesy effect. This is a very effective scale when wishing to play with a Bluesy sound. Note that this soloing scale can be played in both a major or minor key context (band is in major or minor); this is one of the magic qualities of this Blues scale—making it the most common scale used in improvising.

Ex. 3.2

Structure in Improvisation

A third approach is structural in nature. There are many standard short Blues phrases (commonly called licks or riffs), which, when repeated in a logical manner can produce great Blues solos. Below are examples of characteristic Blues licks over a simple repeated left hand bass pattern. They're all written in the key of C. Note that the choice of notes are derived from the major and minor Blues scales. Learning these will give you a basic lick vocabulary to work with as we start to study how phrasing works within Blues. Each lick is four measures long, played twice (for a total of eight measures). Note that from exercise 3.7 on include some possible variations on the basic lick.

Chorus Forms

Whatever happens in the first four measures of a chorus is labeled **A**. **A** becomes your main melody idea (also known as a ***Riff*** or ***Motif***) for the rest of the 12 measures. When **A** is seen again, it is directing you to repeat the first four measures in their entirety. Our first chorus form is **A A A**. The first four measures are stated and labeled **A**. Over the next four measures the **A** is repeated, and over the final four measures the **A** is repeated. Detailed below is an example of the 12 bar Blues progression separated into three equal sections of four measures.

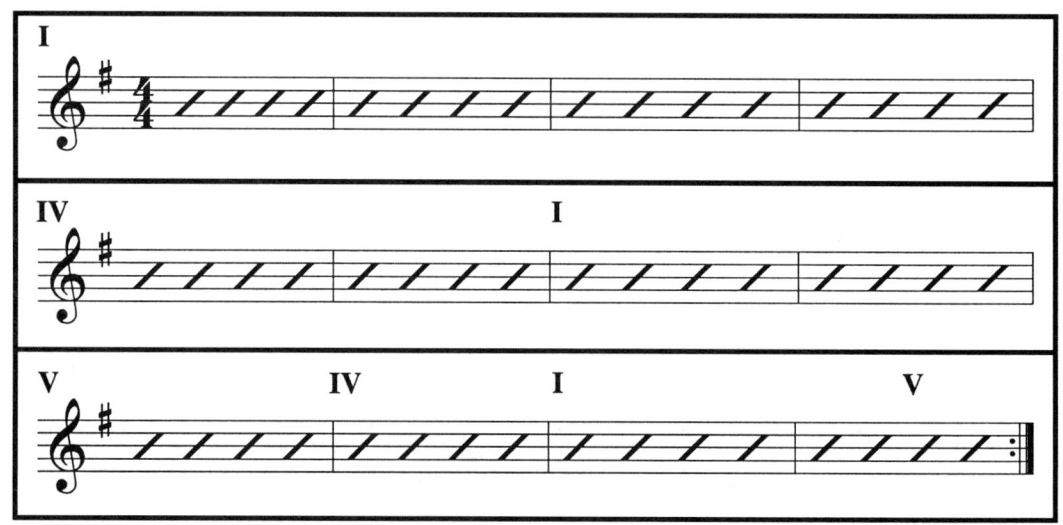

The block form of above looks like the diagram below. We'll use block diagrams for all following examples.

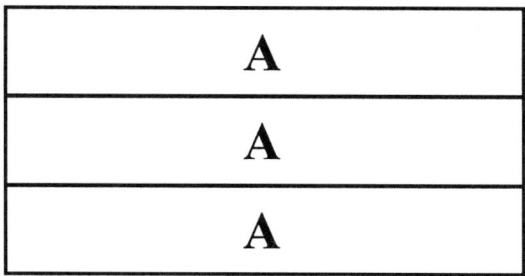

Detailed below is an example of the **A A A** chorus form. Note that the E used in the main lick (as presented on the first line) on the **IV7** chord (F7) has been changed to E♭ to match the flat 7th of the **IV7** chord. This is not required, though it matches the chord change a little better. Try playing it as written once and then play E natural on the **IV7** chord to see which version you like. Both are OK.

It is also common to use smaller **A**'s (2 measure), in essence, making an **AA AA AA** format. This is demonstrated below.

A	A
A	A
A	A

A A A (or **AA AA AA**) is great for the opening of an instrumental. It helps set the mood with a repetitive melody, leaving much room for the soloist to build upon as he or she progresses through a song. This repetition also allows the listener to join in. You play the first **A** to present the melody to the listener. At the first repeat the listener is groovin' along with you. The last repeat the listener is hummin' with you. This is what chorus forms do, engage the listener! It allows the listener to join in your conversation and brings them into the music.

So far, each repeat of **A** has been an exact repeat except for changing the harmony note E to E♭ in measures 5 and 6. At each repeat you can change the line more substantially to add interest. After changing a presented line, the listener will notice the change. The best solos are the ones that keep a remnant of the original idea so that the listener can relate to what you are doing and the changes you are making. When a repeat of a line has changes, but does not stray too far from the original, it is labeled with a variation number. The example below has two variations of the main melody, making it an **A A^1 A^2** chorus form.

A
A^1
A^2

A A B Chorus Form

B represents something different from **A**. **B** is not special in any way other that it is a change from the **A** material. The first four measures are stated and labeled **A**. Over the next four measures the **A** is repeated, and over the final four measures the **B** is stated. **B** will give the chorus the sense of completion—bringing it home. **A A B** is commonly the form used for vocals.

Standard 12 Bar Blues Vocal Verse
I7 – Walkin' down the cellblock, with my head hung low.
IV7 – Walkin' down the cellblock, with my head hung low.
V7 – I just killed my woman's boyfriend, and I'm headed to death row.

Detailed below is an example of the **A A B** chorus form.

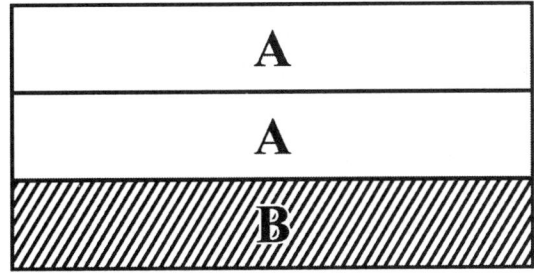

33 Ex. 3.18

As in the **AA AA AA** chorus form before, you can double the **A**'s in the first eight measures (if your lick is two measures or less in length). This is demonstrated below.

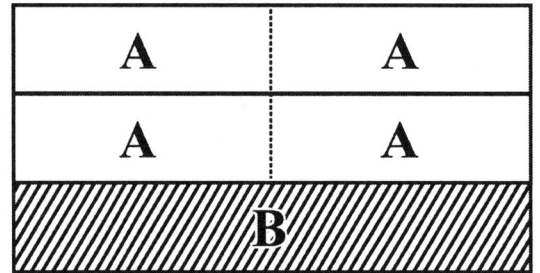

34 Ex. 3.19

A B/A C Chorus Form
A B/A C is our most active chorus form. Like before, **A** states your main theme. **B** is two measures in length (**IV7** Chord) and is a departure from **A**. The next two measures are the **I7** chord, and will be a repeat of **A** material. The final four measures are **C** and is a departure from both **A** and **B** material. Like the **B** in the **A A B** chorus form, this **C** will give the chorus the sense of completion—bringing it home. The **A B/A C** chorus form is demonstrated below.

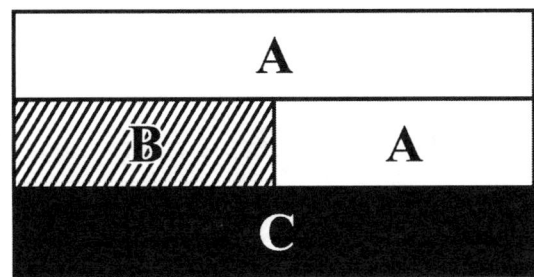

Since the repeat of **A** is only two measures in length, let's make **A** two measures for the opening and play it twice to fill up the four measures. The **A B/A C** chorus form is demonstrated below.

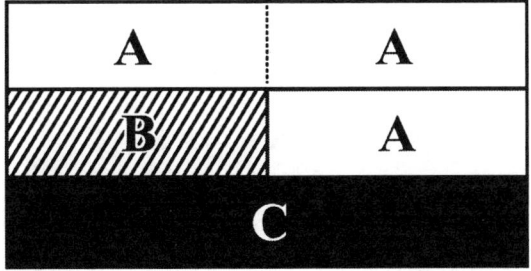

Applying Chorus Forms

How do you become a great soloist in the Blues?… by studying great soloists in the Blues. I have given you a start with some basic Blues piano licks. It's now your turn to listen to great players of Blues piano like Otis Spann and Pinetop Perkins and learn their solos. As you study each lick, place each lick into context by placing them into what we consider good phrasing, using Chorus Forms. As an exercise in this, take each of the licks I have presented to you (examples 3.3 to 3.20) and try to play them in each Chorus Form type (**A A A**, **A A B** & **A B/A C**).

Once you have accomplished this, pick a Blues piano song that you like and learn one of the licks that sounded good to you. First figure out the notes, then work on the rhythm. Listen to where the lick starts in time. Not all licks will start on the downbeat of a measure (beat one). Sometimes a lick will have a pickup (a pickup is a grouping of notes that starts before the measure to introduce a lick) or will start slightly after the downbeat. Be aware of where the lick starts in time so that you know where to place it when applying the Chorus Forms in your improvising. After you are confident with the lick and its timing, try the lick in each of the Chorus Form options (**A A A**, **A A B** & **A B/A C**). Practice for success by placing the licks you learn into the context of how you would play on stage.

You may find it is easier to just play the right hand (the hand that's playing the lick and improvising) without the left hand. You can do this with a jam track. A jam track is a recording of a band playing a Blues groove without a soloist—very much like your left hand without the right hand soloing. I highly recommend purchasing *Blues Keyboard Play-Along Trax* book and CD (MB21062BCD) published by Mel Bay Publications. This presents multiple play-along tracks for you to choose from to employ this concept.

Chapter 4 – Openings, Endings and Breaks

When playing with other musicians you'll need to be familiar with some common ways to open and close a song as well as deal with any stops in the music, called breaks. Let's start with how to open a song.

The first example of opening a song we've already done many times in this book—from the **I**. To start "**From the I**" simply means to play from the beginning of the form. Count in… and away you go.

Starting "**From the V**" is also very common. When doing this intro you (and the band if they play along with you) will start from the 9th measure of the Blues progression as a 4 measure intro. This is demonstrated below.

Ex. 4.1

Another very common way to start is "**From the Turnaround**." When doing this intro you (and the band if they play along with you) will start from the 11th measure of the Blues progression as a 2 measure intro.

Ex. 4.2

Breaks (Stop Time)

The use of a break, also called **Stop Time** or **Break Time**, is a great way to add excitement to a song. The 12 bar Blues progression can get too repetitive sometimes—the break does a great job to… well, break things up!

The first of our two break examples uses a common break lick. Notice the build-up at the 4th measure to lead strongly to chord change (into the **IV7** chord). It is assumed that someone is soloing in the rest area. This could be you (right hand), or another instrument.

Ex. 4.3

Our second most common way to perform a break is to play a chord on the downbeat of each measure.

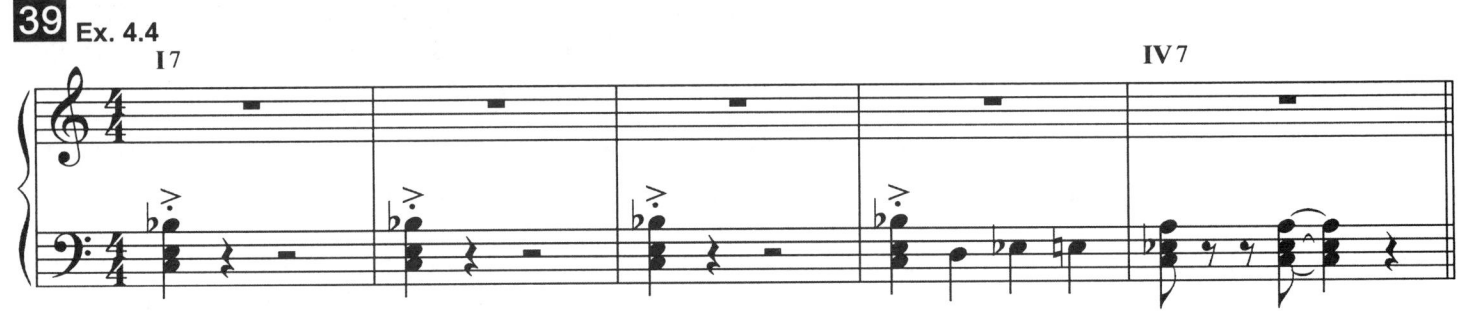

Ex. 4.4

Endings

There are as many, if not more, ways to end a song as there are to open a song. Before we dig into our first example, note that there are two common devices used on endings. A ***Ritard*** is the gradual slowing down at the ending lick. The slow down can be a dramatic or very subtle decrease in tempo. A ***Straight Eighth*** ending would take a normally swung groove and play it straight (no swing) at the ending. These are both nice ways to add a special element to the ending of a song.

The most common place to end a song is to have the band break on the downbeat of the 11th measure. You, or the soloist—or the entire band, then plays an ending lick. After the ending lick the band comes back in to play ending chords. In most of our examples these chords move in a chromatic motion to the **I** chord. Whether you play the **I** chord as a 7th, 9th or other extended chord is up to you on how you want that last chord to sound. It's also common to have the band do a strong hit to completely end the song.

Note: In the following examples I've written a different figure in the left hand. This is a comping (accompaniment) pattern based on the Charleston Rhythm in Example 2.4. You can use this pattern when you're soloing in a band situation and the tempo or the texture of the music makes our other left hand patterns too heavy for the situation. Also note that the short-long element of the pattern is very important. The symbol over the last chord is called a ***Fermata***. When the fermata is present you hold the last chord until the bandleader (you if you're playing alone) signals to stop.

Ex. 4.5

Another common way to end is to break on the 10th measure (**IV7** chord) for one measure and then go into an ending lick. The example below demonstrates the same ending lick as Example 4.5 with the addition of the break on the **IV7** chord.

Ex. 4.6

Lastly, it's not uncommon to play the last four measures for a total of three times—ending on the last repeat.

42 Ex. 4.7

Chapter 5 – **Blues Organ**

I like to say that the Piano and Organ have only one thing in common: a keyboard. Other than that, they really are two entirely different instruments. Piano is technically a percussion instrument because sound is generated when a hammer strikes a string. The organ is not. It can sustain notes as long as you hold down a key. And the organ is not touch sensitive. You can strike the keyboard as hard as you want and it's not going to make any difference. So, although they both share the keyboard, the approach to the two instruments is quite different.

In the context of the Blues, the organ either solos or is used for coloration. The original Hammond organ is not sensitive to touch, so I advise you to turn off the touch sensitivity on your synthesizer's organ patches. The organ, however, does have a volume control operated by a foot pedal. If you have a continuous control pedal, plug it in and use it musically—don't just pump it up and down with the beat. And for you Hammond purists, the pedal is really an expression control. That is, it varies the volume and tone at the same time (to be technical, it acts like the loudness switch on your stereo, the low and high ends don't diminish in volume anywhere near as much as do the midrange frequencies when you back it off).

Note that the classic Hammond sound requires a Leslie tone cabinet. Many models were made, but the classic is the model 122 or 147. This large wooden box (weighing in at around 150 lbs.) not only colors the tone as it goes through its tube amplifier to the 15 inch speaker and horn, but does another neat trick. With the flip of a switch the horn can rotate either at slow or fast speed as the rotating drum around the downward facing woofer spins in the opposite direction. It's all very amusing, but the point is, when this thing revs up, sound is being thrown all over the place and it's like nothing else on the market. So you can hold down one note on the organ and create a splash by merely turning the speaker from slow (or stopped) to fast. On your synthesizer you'll probably be able to do this by moving the modulation control. Check it out.

Now back to the Hammond. The original has drawbars, nine actual metal and plastic sliders that you pull out from under the top cover of the organ to make sound. If they're all in, there's no sound, if you pull three out, you'll get all three sounding when you press any key. The drawbars control tones that are generally an octave or fifth apart from each other. On some synthesizers there may be sliders to control these tones, which is great because moving the drawbars in and out as you play results in a lot of exciting sound changes. Even if your machine doesn't have this, just be aware that the tone of the organ can go from mellow (i.e. mostly fundamental frequencies) to rocking (low, mids and highs all together).

Like a lot of things, experience is the best teacher. If you want to know more about the Hammond organ, get some recordings by: Jimmy Smith, Jack McDuff, Jimmy McGriff (*Greatest Hits* on the Blue Note label). On the bluesier side get recordings by: Billy Preston, Ron Levy and Bruce Katz. These provide good examples of the organ in the Blues genre.

Note: The late, great Jimmy Smith was the major figure in the development of the modern Hammond organ sound in Jazz *and* Blues. Check out a few of his classic blues cuts: "Bashin," "T-Bone Steak," "Got My Mojo Workin'," "Organ Grinder Swing," "I'll Drink to That," and "Back at the Chicken Shack" among others.

On the next page I've diagrammed some of the common Hammond drawbar settings. I've demonstrated the sounds with chorus (which is a switch on the organ that feeds back the original sound slightly delayed with the original to produce a vibrating effect) both on and off. Also I've played these examples with the Leslie speaker stopped and then rotating fast (there is a slow setting on the Leslie, but due to the limited technology of the day, you can either have Slow and Fast or off and Fast. I'm one of those who prefer the latter).

If you are a lucky Hammond organ owner, these settings will be useful to you. If you aren't, but will be playing organ parts on a synth, I hope this gives you a sound reference for the common organ settings. You'll probably find patches on your machine that lie in the general ballpark. A good website that will tell you more about this fascinating subject is http://theatreorgans.com/hammond/faq/.

Typical Drawbar Settings:

43 Jimmy Smith — 888 000 000 – Percussion: On, Soft, Fast, Third (A solo tone)
44 Groove Holmes — 888 000 008   (Another solo tone)
45 Booker T. 1 — 888 800 000
46 Booker T. 2 — 888 800 000 – Percussion: On, Soft, Fast, Second (One of his solo tones—always with Chorus Off)
47 Rock — 688 600 000
48 Jazz — 800 000 008   (A mellow jazz setting)
49 Squabble — 800 005 678   (Used with Chorus On, Leslie Fast to play octave chords)
50 Chords — 808 000 008   (Used for—Chords!)
51 Gospel 1 — 808 808 008   (Chorus On and Leslie Fast and you're in church!)
52 Gospel 2 — 800 808 008   (Ditto)
53 Diagonal — 876 543 210
54 Curved — 875 313 578
55 Full Organ — 888 888 888   (Use this when they say "Pull out all the stops!")
56 Change from Jazz to Full Organ (Check out the dramatic change in tone)

The above settings will work for the upper manual of the Hammond organ, which is usually played by the right hand. The lower manual is used either for bass lines or chording. A good bass setting is: **838 000 000** and a good chord setting is usually **008 400 000**.

Two-Handed Music Examples

Below are some two-handed Organ exercises in the 12 Bar Blues form. Note that we will move out of the key of C for some of these exercises. When starting an example, look at the left hand side of where the clef resides. If you see a sharp on a line (#), every note on that line throughout the example should be raised by one half step. When you see a natural sign (♮) precede a note, that note, and every other note on the same line within that measure is to be played as written, not sharped or flatted. The same rule applies for flats (but in the case of flats, the note will be lowered by a half step). This is called a **Key Signature** and is used to cleanly represent new keys.

This exercise in G is in straight time. This means it's to be played as written and not swung. Or, if you like, with very little swing. This is pretty much the part for Jimmie Smith's famous recording of "I Got My Mojo Workin'." Notice that your left hand is playing the bass line. If you have no bass player, or are playing in the classic Organ Jazz style, you're the bassist! By the way, this is a standard part of Organ playing. It's often called **Kicking Bass**. Why "kicking bass"? The Hammond has a set of bass pedals on the floor under the two manuals. While most Organ Bass is done on the lower (left-hand) manual, it is not uncommon to accent or double certain bass notes with bass notes on the pedals. The audience sees this of course and assumes you're playing the entire bass line with your left foot. This is not exactly true.

Here is a blues in the key of C on the organ with a **Walking Bass Line**. This refers to a bass line made up of quarter notes, sometimes moving up or down the scale, hence "walking." For the right hand use the Jimmy Smith setting above. For the left use the bass line setting. By the way, notice the harmonic complexity of this Blues. It's still a Blues, but the bass line implies a more elaborate chord structure. These chords still follow the general pattern of our three chord Blues, but add more nuance and subtlety. This exercise is to be played "swing style."

58 Ex. 5.2

This is a two-chord jam in G. Straight time again.

59 Ex. 5.3

45

This final example is close to the iconic organ riff in Booker T's "Green Onions." Play it in swing style with both hands on one manual using the Booker T. registration with Leslie stopped and no chorus.

60 Ex. 5.4

61 Common Organ Techniques

Here are a few common organ techniques. Below are demonstrated various *Slides* or *Glissandi* as they're called. You'll find it an effective way to enter or end a phrase. They can be done with the finger(s) or palm of the right hand. You may also use the left hand to do the slide and switch to the right hand to play the actual note.

Ex. 5.5

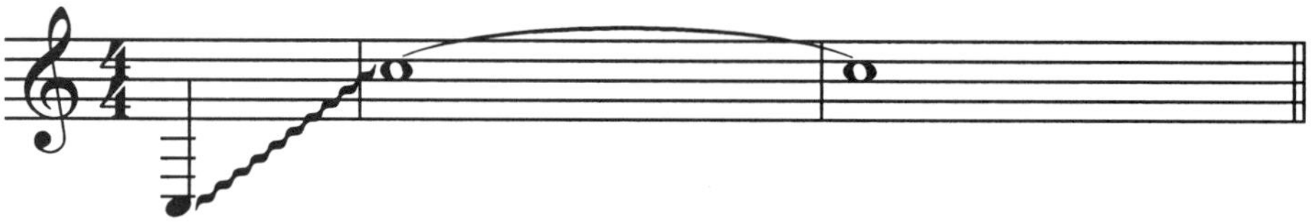

Ex. 5.6

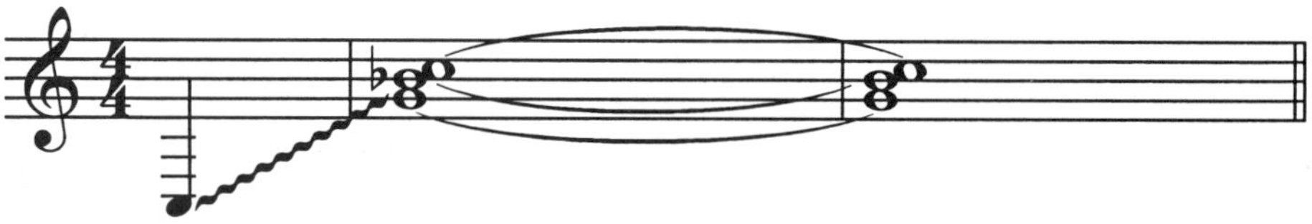

Ex. 5.7

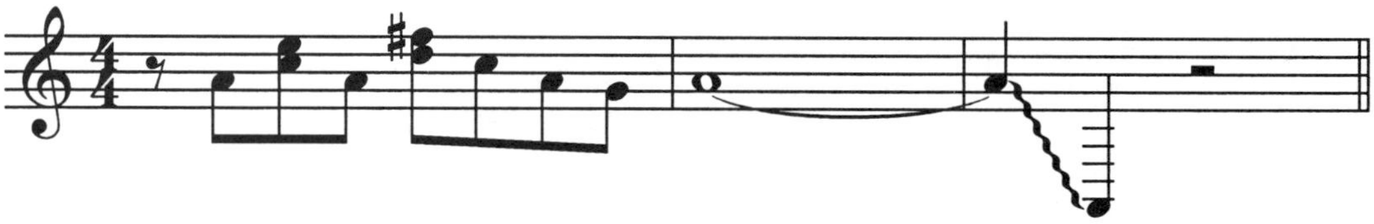

46

This final example is a common organ device where you trill between 2 notes, usually a minor third apart.

Ex. 5.8

Final Thoughts

That brings us to the end of this book. I hope you enjoyed and benefited from the ideas in this book. Remember to keep practicing and enjoy your time at the keyboard. I highly recommend purchasing *Blues Keyboard Play-Along Trax (21062BCD)*. This companion book and CD will feature full-length band tracks that you can play along with to practice your right hand improvising. After these two books you're ready to move to the next book within the *School of the Blues Lesson Series* called *Blues Keyboard, Level 2 (21061BCD)*. In this second book we'll continue our blues keyboard studies.

Please visit our web site at www.schooloftheblues.com for information on lessons and workshops.

Recommended Listening

Below are some "must have" albums that personify what we've been studying. Study these recordings just like you studied this book.

Piano

Artist	Recording	Label
Professor Longhair	Fess: Anthology	Rhino
Meade Lux Lewis	The Blues Piano Artistry of Meade Lux Lewis	Ojc
Albert Ammons	The Boogie Woogie Trio, Vols. 1-2	Storyville Records
Otis Spann	Otis Spann Is the Blues	Candid Records
James Booker	New Orleans Piano Wizard: Live!	Rounder
Memphis Slim	The Gate of the Horn	Collectables
Various	Atlantic Blues Piano	Atlantic

Organ

Artist	Recording	Label
Jimmy McGriff	Jimmy McGriff - Greatest Hits	Blue Note
	The Starting Five	Milestone
Jimmy Smith	The Sermon!	Blue Note
	The Best of Jimmy Smith: The Blue Note Years	Blue Note
Billy Preston	Billy's Bag	Rpm
	The Wildest Organ in Town!/Club Meeting	EMI Int'l

Thanks To...

I'd like to thank David Barrett and the folks at the School of the Blues for the opportunity to share my music with a wider audience through these books. Also thanks to my wife Jeanne and my daughter Sara for their inspiration and support.

I would also like to thank the following people for their contribution to this book and recording.

- Producer, Editor & Co-Author – David Barrett
- Proof Readers – Jeanne Czarnecki and Dennis Carelli
- Photography – Dave Lepori Photography in San Jose, California

School of the Blues Staff
Front Row (L-R): Frank De Rose, John Garcia and Kevin Coggins
Back Row (L-R): Steve Czarnecki and David Barrett